Jude
the Librarian
Fairy

Join the **Rainbow Magic Reading Challenge!**

ead the story and collect your fairy points to climb the
Reading Rainbow at the back of the book.

This book is worth 2 stars.

For Terri, the coolest librarian I know

Special thanks to
Rachel Elliot

ORCHARD BOOKS

First published in Great Britain in 2021 by The Watts Publishing Group Limited

1 3 5 7 9 10 8 6 4 2

© 2021 Rainbow Magic Limited.
© 2021 HIT Entertainment Limited.
Illustrations © 2021 The Watts Publishing Group Limited.

A CIP catalogue record for this book is available from the British Library.

ISBN 978 1 40835 772 9

Printed and bound in Great Britain by Clays Ltd, Elcograf S.p.A

The paper and board used in this book are made from wood from responsible sources

Orchard Books
An imprint of Hachette Children's Group
Part of The Watts Publishing Group Limited
Carmelite House, 50 Victoria Embankment, London EC4Y 0DZ

An Hachette UK Company
www.hachette.co.uk
www.hachettechildrens.co.uk

Jude
the Librarian
Fairy

By Daisy Meadows

ORCHARD

www.orchardseriesbooks.co.uk

Fairyland
Palace

Fairyland Library

Wetherbury Library

Contents

Story One:
The Lucky Library Stamp

Chapter One: A Big Day for Wetherbury   11
Chapter Two: Magic in a Book   19
Chapter Three: Word Whirl   29
Chapter Four: What Lydia Heard   39
Chapter Five: Saved by a Sneeze   49

Story Two:
The Radiant Reading Glasses

Chapter Six: The Moat Mission   61
Chapter Seven: Pixies to the Rescue   73
Chapter Eight: The Worst Librarian Ever   81
Chapter Nine: Testing Jack Frost   89
Chapter Ten: A Little Help from Alana Yarn   97

Story Three:
The Brilliant Bookmark

Chapter Eleven: Mops and Magic   111
Chapter Twelve: Disaster Strikes   119
Chapter Thirteen: Through the Roof   127
Chapter Fourteen: The Goblin Tree   135
Chapter Fifteen: Fairy First Aid   145

Jack Frost's Spell

Don't throw books – don't shout or run.
Librarians are not much fun!
I'm fed up with the silly fools,
And I don't care about their rules.

I'm Jack Frost! The boss! The star!
I'm worth much more than bookworms are.
With Jude's magic in my hand,
Her boring rules will soon be banned!

Story One
The Lucky Library Stamp

Chapter One
A Big Day for Wetherbury

"Today's the day!" said Kirsty, bouncing out of bed. "Wetherbury's brand-new library is opening at last. Wake up, sleepyhead!"

She jumped on top of the mound of blankets on the spare bed. The mound gave a squeal of laughter and her best friend Rachel Walker sat up.

"I don't need an alarm clock with you around," she said, grinning.

Just then, Kirsty's mum came in with a pile of clean clothes.

"Good morning, girls," she said. "Please get dressed and come downstairs. Dad's cooking a splendid breakfast to make sure that you will have lots of energy to enjoy your big day."

"Thanks, Mum," said Kirsty. "It's a big day for everyone."

"That's true," said Mrs Tate, as she put the clothes away. "I think that almost everyone in the village did something to help raise money for the new library."

"We had lots of fun making cakes and lemonade for our street-market stall," said Rachel.

"Yes," said Kirsty, remembering. "We sold every single cake, and I was sorry, because they were so yummy I could have eaten them all myself!"

Laughing, the girls put on their clothes. Mrs Tate went back downstairs, and the girls soon joined her. Kirsty's dad was already serving up plates of scrambled eggs, beans, sausages, bacon and toast.

"I wish that we had a library opening every day, if this is the kind of breakfast we get," said Mrs Tate, smiling at the girls.

"So what's the plan today?" asked Mr Tate, pouring a glass of orange juice for everyone.

"All the people who raised money for the library have been invited to look around before it opens to the public," said Kirsty.

"Best of all, Alana Yarn is going to be there," Rachel added.

"Isn't she one of your favourite authors?" asked Mrs Tate.

The girls nodded.

"After the fundraisers have explored, Alana will cut the ribbon and declare the library open," said Kirsty.

"And the reading challenge medals are

going to be awarded, and there will be cakes and a raffle," said Rachel, counting things off on her fingers. "I can't wait."

A short time later, the girls were walking into the brand-new library. A few of the other fundraisers were already inside, browsing through the shelves.

"Wow, this is even better than I imagined," said Kirsty.

The space was very small, but every detail was perfect. The walls were decorated with brightly coloured murals. The children's cosy corner had bean bags and a box of cuddly toys for babies. Best of all, the shelves were filled with shiny new books.

"Welcome," said the librarian, flicking her long, curly blonde hair back over her shoulder. "Thank you for helping us to give Wetherbury this beautiful library."

"Oh my goodness," said Rachel in delight. "Look who's here . . ."

Alana Yarn was sitting in a big yellow armchair in the middle of the library.

Chapter Two
Magic in a Book

Alana Yarn waved when she saw the girls. They stepped forward, feeling dizzy with excitement.

"Don't I remember you both from the Storytelling Festival?" she said.

"Yes, it was brilliant," said Rachel. "It got everyone feeling really excited about books and stories."

"Wetherbury Library will carry on that good work," said Alana. "Libraries really are magical places. A small room like this can contain thousands of people, hundreds of worlds."

Rachel and Kirsty shared a secret smile. They knew more about magic than Alana Yarn could have guessed. Together, they had made friends with the fairies and had many incredible adventures.

"Wow, I can't believe she remembers us," Kirsty whispered.

The librarian spoke to the little group of people who had gathered.

"We have a wonderful day planned," she said. "There will be craft activities, plenty to eat and drink, and some readings with Alana Yarn. Children who have completed the reading challenge will be able to collect their medals. And don't forget to pick up a library card. But first, this is your chance to look around. Have fun exploring your new library."

The best friends skipped over to the children's corner. Rachel ran her fingers along the colourful shelves.

"It's hard to choose," she said. "All the books look so amazing. Mysteries, magic, talking animals, funny books, true stories

. . . which one shall I pick?"

"How about that one?" said Kirsty in a low, excited voice.

She pointed to an orange-covered book at the end of a shelf. Tiny, glowing sparkles were shooting across it.

"It's magic," whispered Rachel.

She reached out and picked up the book. It fell open in her hands, and out fluttered a tiny fairy. She was wearing a

pair of soft, grey trousers with a flowered
blouse, and her filmy wings were pale
orange.

"Hello, girls," she whispered. "When I
heard that you had helped to set up a
library, I had to come and say hello. I'm
Jude the Librarian Fairy, and it's my job
to watch over librarians and to help them
keep libraries running smoothly."

"Welcome," said
Kirsty. "Are you
going to be
watching over
our library too?"
Jude nodded,
making her
brown hair
bounce merrily in
its ponytail. "I make

sure that books are always available and well looked after, and that everyone has a chance to read something they love."

"What a lovely job," said Rachel. "It must be wonderful to be surrounded by books all day."

"It's where I feel happiest," said Jude, smiling. "I spend most of my spare time in the Fairyland 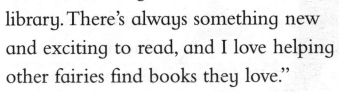 library. There's always something new and exciting to read, and I love helping other fairies find books they love."

"Someone's coming," said Kirsty.

Quickly, Jude slipped into the pocket

of Rachel's T-shirt. The girls went over to the window.

"Lydia the Reading Fairy told me about her adventure with you," Jude said. "Then the Storybook Fairies told me about everything you had done for them. I've been really looking forward to meeting you."

"Today was always going to be amazing," said Rachel. "But now you're here, it's absolutely fantastic."

At that moment, there was a loud

CRASH!

"That came from the other side of the library," said Kirsty. "Come on!"

Chapter Three
Word Whirl

The girls hurried to see what had happened. A shelf had been knocked over, and books were scattered everywhere. The librarian was on her hands and knees, picking them up.

"What happened?" asked Kirsty, kneeling down to help.

"Some children were getting a bit too excited," said the librarian. "They knocked the shelf over by accident. Luckily, no one was hurt."

Just then, they heard running footsteps.

"Walk, please," the librarian called out.

"I'll ask them to come back and help tidy up," said Rachel.

She followed the sound of scampering feet, and found a group of boys emptying the toy boxes in the children's corner.

"Stop that!" said Rachel. "It's not fair to expect other people to clear up after you. I've come to ask you to help tidy up the mess you made over there."

The boys huddled together and squawked with laughter. Kirsty came up behind Rachel.

"Please be quiet," she said. "You're spoiling things for everyone else."

"You can't tell us what to do," one of the boys shouted.

"These naughty boys are breaking too many library rules," said Jude, peeping out of Rachel's pocket. "I have a little spell that will remind them about being respectful to others."

She raised her wand, and Rachel and Kirsty waited, expecting to see the boys start behaving. But they were making more noise than ever.

"How long does the spell take to work?" asked Kirsty.

"It should have worked straight away," Jude said, looking confused.

She tapped her wand on her hand and then waved it again. The boys jumped up and started pulling books from the shelf and putting them back in the wrong places. Just then, Rachel noticed something.

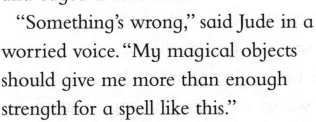

"Look at their enormous feet," she whispered. "They're green."

"Goblins," said Kirsty with a groan.

One of the goblins heard her and edged a little closer.

"Something's wrong," said Jude in a worried voice. "My magical objects should give me more than enough strength for a spell like this."

The goblin smiled and started cackling with laughter.

"Your silly objects will never help you again," he squawked. "They have a new owner now."

Rachel and Kirsty stared at him in shock.

"What does he mean?" asked Jude in a trembling voice.

"Oh, Jude," said Rachel. "I think that Jack Frost has stolen your magical objects!"

Jude clutched the edge of Rachel's pocket.

"I have to get back to Fairyland and check," she cried.

"Let us come with you," said Kirsty at once. "We can help."

"We'll have to find a quiet place," said Rachel, looking around. "Let's be quick – the library's getting busier every minute."

The girls ducked out of sight behind a shelf, and Jude fluttered out of Rachel's pocket. She waved her wand and there was a ruffling sound, like the pages of a book turning very quickly.

"Oh," whispered Kirsty in awe.

A spiral of printed words came from the tip of the wand, spinning faster and faster, and lifting the girls into the air. As they were lifted up, Rachel and Kirsty shrank to fairy size and felt their wings start to open. Black letters looped and coiled around them.

"I feel as if I'm inside a book," Rachel said, laughing as the letters wound around her arms and legs.

Slowly, the letters faded to grey and then disappeared. The girls were standing in a pool of sunlight under an arched glass ceiling. All around, the walls were lined with books. At once, Jude darted

over to a polished wooden desk.

"I know this place," said Kirsty in delight. "We're in the Fairyland Library."

Chapter Four
What Lydia Heard

Rachel and Kirsty had first visited the Fairyland Library with the Storybook Fairies. It was one of the most peaceful places in Fairyland, filled with comfortable armchairs and thousands of magical books, and they loved it. They gazed around as Jude pulled open a drawer in the desk.

"Oh no," she cried. "You were right. My magical objects have been stolen."

She sank on to a chair. Rachel and Kirsty hurried over and put their arms around her. The open desk drawer was lined with purple velvet, and there were three sad little dents where the magical objects had been.

"What do they do?" asked Kirsty.

"The lucky library stamp makes sure that everyone follows the rules of the library," Jude explained. "The radiant reading glasses help librarians to be well organised, and the brilliant bookmark keeps all the books in the right places on the shelves. Without them, librarians all over the world will find it impossible to do their job. Libraries will be in chaos, and all the wonderful things that librarians do will come to an end."

"I don't even want to imagine a world without librarians in it," said Rachel. "They know so much about books, and they're so kind and clever."

"And they're always there to listen if you need someone to talk to," added Kirsty. "We have to get those magical

41

objects back where they belong."

"But where shall we start looking?" asked Jude.

"I think I can help you with that," said a familiar voice.

Lydia the Reading Fairy came fluttering towards them, looking upset. Rachel and Kirsty hugged her tightly.

"It's lovely to see you, Lydia," said Rachel. "Can you tell us what happened here?"

"Jack Frost came in about half an hour ago," Lydia said. "He pretended to want a rare book from the furthest shelves. When I went to fetch it, three goblins pushed me into a storage cupboard. I've only just managed to get out."

"Oh, Lydia, you poor thing," said Rachel.

"I know why he's done this," said Jude. "He visited the library yesterday, and he was being very noisy and messy. I asked him to speak more quietly and to pick up his litter from the floor. I expect this is his way of getting his own back."

"I heard the goblins talking about where to hide the magical objects," said Lydia. "One of them said he was going to one of the oldest libraries in the world."

Jude looked happier.

"That could be the City Library," she said. "Rachel, Kirsty, please will you come with me and try to get my things back?"

"Of course we will," said Rachel and Kirsty together.

"I'll stay here and tidy up," said Lydia. "The goblins left an awful mess."

Jude waved her wand. At once, a glittering, pale-blue mist swirled upwards from the ground until it completely surrounded the three fairies. For a moment, Rachel and Kirsty could see nothing. Then the mist cleared.

"Welcome to the City Library,"

whispered Jude.

The three fairies were looking down from near the top of a high bookcase.

"Oh my goodness," said Kirsty. "This is the most ancient room I've ever seen."

Wooden panels on every wall were carved with eagles, lions, unicorns and stags. The floor was made of dark, polished wood. People were sitting at long oak tables in the middle of the room, reading large, old books. The only sounds were the creaking floorboards and the low swish of turning pages.

"Let's start looking," said Rachel.

She rose into the air and fluttered towards the ceiling. Kirsty and Jude followed her closely.

"There are lots of narrow passageways, tiny rooms and hidden nooks and crannies in this old building," said Jude, looking anxious. "I love it here, but it's going to be really, really hard to find a hiding goblin."

Chapter Five
Saved by a Sneeze

The fairies flew for miles. They went back and forth along the passageways and through the higgledy-piggledy rooms. They swooped under bookcases and in and out of tightly packed aisles. They split up and went over and over the same areas. At last they met up on a table in an empty room.

"No luck," said Kirsty. "All I've seen is people breaking the rules of the library."

"Me too," said Rachel. "People have been talking in loud voices and eating around the books."

"I saw people disobeying the librarians and writing in books," Jude added. "I even saw a librarian lose his temper with a visitor. Things are going badly wrong."

"Maybe the goblin changed his mind," said Rachel.

She stretched and arched her back . . . and then gasped.

"Look up," she whispered.

The goblin was perching on top of

the tallest bookcase, still dressed as a boy.
When the fairies saw him, he let out a
fierce squawk. Then he swung down the
bookcase like a monkey and darted out
of the room.

"Fly!" Kirsty shouted.

It was a wild chase. The goblin led the
fairies through forests of chair legs and
mountains of piled-up books. He tumbled
down winding stairways and romped
across tables.

"He's going down to the basement,"
Jude called out.
"There's no way out
of there – it's where all
the oldest books are
kept."

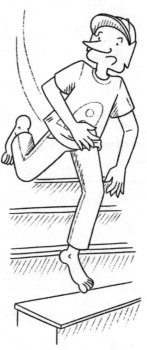

"Maybe we can stop
him for long enough
to talk to him," said
Kirsty, panting.

In the basement, the
goblin showed no sign
of slowing down. He
pelted along the aisles.

He bumped into shelves and sent old books crashing down. Clouds of dust rose up as they slammed to the floor.

"He's going to ruin these beautiful books," cried Jude.

But at that moment, the goblin stopped running and froze. The fairies stopped too, hovering behind him.

"Are you OK?" Rachel asked.

"Ah – ah – ah – CHOO!" spluttered the goblin. "Help! AH-CHOO! AH-CHOO! AH-CHOO!"

"It's the dust," said Kirsty, pulling her handkerchief from her pocket. "It's gone right up his nose. Here, borrow this."

The goblin sneezed helplessly into Kirsty's tiny little handkerchief. He stumbled sideways and bumped into another shelf. More books fell down and more dust rose up.

"AH-CHOO!" the goblin snorted.
"AH-CHOO! AH-CHOO!"

His sneezes shook his whole body,
and his eyes streamed with tears. As he
lurched forwards, a shiny rubber stamp
fell out of his pocket.

"My lucky library stamp," Jude exclaimed. "Hurray!"

Rachel was closest, and she zoomed to pick it up. As soon as she handed it to Jude, the stamp shrank to fairy size.

Jude tapped the goblin's head with her wand. He stopped sneezing at once, and vanished in a flurry of sparkles.

"I've sent him back to the goblin village," Jude said. "That way, Jack Frost won't find out straight away that I've got the lucky library stamp back."

"It might give us time to find out where the radiant reading glasses and the brilliant bookmark are," said Kirsty.

"Let's get your stamp back to the Fairyland Library where it belongs," said Rachel.

"Yes," said Kirsty. "And then we should go straight to the Ice Castle. Together, we're going to foil Jack Frost's plan!"

Story Two
The Radiant
Reading Glasses

Chapter Six
The Moat Mission

When Rachel, Kirsty and Jude flew back
into the Fairyland Library, they found
Lydia sorting through the last muddled-
up pile of books. When she saw them,
she jumped up and down, clapping her
hands.

"You look happy," she said. "Did you

get your objects back?"

"We made a good start," said Jude, smiling. "The lucky library stamp can return to where it belongs."

She placed it in the velvet-lined drawer, but her smile faded as she looked at the two empty spaces.

"We won't stop searching until all your objects are back where they belong," said Kirsty.

"Let's go to the Ice Castle and see what we can find out," said Rachel.

"The goblin I sent to the goblin village will still be on his way there," said Jude. "If we hurry, we might be able to find the missing objects before he tells Jack Frost that I've got the lucky library stamp back."

Jude led Rachel and Kirsty out of the library and they all rose into the air.

"I've never seen the library from the outside before," said Kirsty.

"It looks like a castle," said Rachel.

The library was made of sand-coloured stone that glowed in the sunlight. It had delicate spires as twisty as unicorn horns.

Crystal windows sparkled on every side.

"It's beautiful," Kirsty whispered to herself. "We won't let Jack Frost spoil this place for everyone."

Soon, the fairies were speeding towards
the Ice Castle. As they got closer, the sky
changed from forget-me-not blue to grim
grey. Then the frozen walls of Jack Frost's
home loomed up in front of them. The
fairies perched on the bare branches of a
nearby tree.

"Look over there," said Kirsty.

Two goblins were standing beside the

moat, yelling at each other. One of them was wearing a scuba diving suit. The other was very tall. He was holding a blue tin box and waving it around as he shouted.

"What are they doing?" asked Rachel.

"It looks as if they're quarrelling about something," said Kirsty. "How can we get closer and find out what's wrong?"

Jude thought for a moment, and then a smile spread across her face.

"The goblins won't talk to fairies," she said. "But they might talk to pixies. Goblins like pixies because they're cheeky and they've got the same pointy ears."

She waved her wand, and flashes of red, green and yellow burst around their heads. Rachel and Kirsty blinked and stared at each other in amazement. Each

of them had shrunk to the size of a pixie.
They were wearing red caps, yellow
trousers and green jackets with the words
'Water Inspector' on them.

"Come on, let's see what they're doing,"

said Jude in a high-pitched pixie voice.

They hurried towards the goblins, who turned as they came closer.

"Water inspectors?" asked the scuba

goblin, peering at their jackets. "What do you need to inspect water for?"

"We have to make sure it's safe," said Kirsty in a serious voice. "Diving into dirty water can make you very poorly."

"Ooh, I don't like being poorly," wailed the scuba goblin. "I knew this was a mistake."

"Why do you want to dive into a freezing cold moat anyway?" Rachel asked.

"I don't," the goblin grumbled. "Jack Frost told us to hide this box, and smarty-pants over there thought it would be a good idea to bury it at the bottom of the moat. Then he said I had to take it down there."

He stuck out his tongue at the tall goblin, whose long nose was bright red and drippy.

"It's not my fault I've got a cold," the tall goblin replied.

He blew his nose into a spotty green handkerchief.

"What's in the box?" asked Kirsty.

The scuba goblin looked around and

put his finger to his lips.

"Something that belongs to a fairy," he whispered. "But don't you dare tell her. Tee hee! She'll never find it down there!"

Chapter Seven
Pixies to the Rescue

Rachel and Kirsty exchanged a worried glance. They felt sure that Jude's objects must be inside the box. Worse still, the goblin was right. They would never get it when it had been buried at the bottom of the moat.

"Don't make yourselves ill by diving

into dirty water," said Rachel. "Let us take the box instead."

"Yes!" said the scuba goblin at once. "That sounds like a brilliant plan. There's no diving in it."

The tall goblin sniffed loudly and held out the box. Jude darted forward to take it.

"Stop!" bellowed a furious voice.

The tall goblin snatched the box back and hugged it to his chest. He darted behind the scuba goblin, trembling. Jack Frost came stomping towards them through the snow.

"I'm sick of you wretched goblins giving away the things that I have rightfully stolen!" he yelled. "What do these puny pixies want?"

"They're here to test the moat for

yucky things," gabbled the scuba goblin.

"The only yucky things around here are you lot," Jack Frost snapped. "Pixies don't belong here at my castle. Buzz off."

"I don't think it's safe to bury the tin at the bottom of the moat," said Rachel.

"Nobody asked what a nosy little pixie

thinks," said Jack Frost.

"Can we at least see what's inside?" asked Kirsty.

Jack Frost glared at her.

"I don't trust pixies," he said. "Why are you so interested in the box?"

"The things inside it don't belong to you," Jude burst out.

Jack Frost pushed his face towards hers until their noses were touching. He squinted at her.

"You want the box for yourself, don't you?" he hissed. "You can't have it, do you hear me? I want to get my own back on that boring, stuck-up Librarian Fairy. Why shouldn't I make a noise or write in books? No one tells me what to do! I'll spoil her precious libraries, starting with that stupid one in Wetherbury."

He snatched the tin and then gave the goblins a hard shove. *SPLASH!* They tumbled backwards into the moat. Jack Frost jabbed his wand into the air and streaks of blue lightning crackled from it. Then, with a loud clap of thunder, he was gone.

"Help!" spluttered the goblins.

Rachel and Kirsty reached out their hands and pulled the soggy goblins out of the water. They squelched off towards the castle without a single "thank you", squabbling about whose fault it all was. The three disguised fairies looked at each other.

"What now?" asked Jude.

"We have to get back to Wetherbury," Kirsty said. "Goodness knows what Jack Frost will already have done to the library."

With a wave of her wand, Jude whisked them into the air. A second later they were standing in the children's corner of the new Wetherbury Library. Rachel and Kirsty were human again, and Jude was back to being a fairy.

"I hope no one noticed us appearing," said Rachel.

"I don't think we need to worry about that," said Kirsty with a groan. "Look at the mess!"

Chapter Eight
The Worst Librarian Ever

The library was in chaos. Books were scattered on the floor, and people were complaining in loud voices.

"I've never seen such a disorganised library."

"It's disgraceful."

The girls saw the nice librarian peering

underneath the shelves. Jude darted under Kirsty's hair.

"Have you lost something?" Rachel asked her. "Can we help you?"

"Oh, girls, I hope so," said the librarian, looking tearful. "Everything is going wrong. I can't find my 'to do' list, and the Reading Challenge medals have gone missing. I don't have time to help anyone, or organise Alana Yarn's book reading. This library opening is turning into a disaster."

Before the girls could reply, someone cleared his throat behind them. When they turned around, they saw a very strange-looking person. He was wearing a smart blue suit, silver-rimmed glasses and a pair of very pointy boots. His spiky hair had been forced into a topknot, but

his spiky beard was the same as ever.
Rachel and Kirsty exchanged a horrified
glance. It was Jack Frost!

"Oh, goodness me," said the librarian,
taking a little step backwards. "How can
I . . . er . . . help you?"

"I'm the new librarian," said Jack

Frost, puffing out his chest. "I'm the best librarian there is. I can do all the librarian stuff, just watch me."

"That's great, I really need an extra pair of hands right now," said the real librarian. "Could you help the people who want to borrow a book?"

"Oh, I'll help them," said Jack Frost with a crafty smile.

"I don't like the way he said that," Kirsty whispered to Rachel. "He's caused all this confusion using Jude's magic."

The librarian turned to the girls.

"Please will you tidy up some of these books while I look for the medals?" she asked.

"Of course we will," said Rachel.

The librarian gave them a little smile and hurried away. Then Jude peered out

from under Kirsty's hair
and let out a horrified
cry at the sight of
Jack Frost.

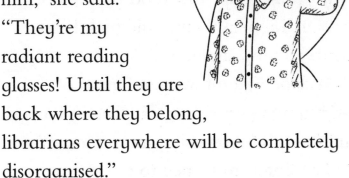

"Those glasses
don't belong to
him," she said.
"They're my
radiant reading
glasses! Until they are
back where they belong,
librarians everywhere will be completely
disorganised."

Jack Frost put his thumb to his nose
and waggled his fingers at the girls. Then
he turned to the queue of people.

"Well, what do you want?" he snapped
at the first gentleman in the queue.

"I'm, er, looking for a book about

birds," the gentleman stuttered.

"Birds?" Jack Frost repeated. "Boring! I don't care about birds. Come back when you've got a more interesting question. Next!"

An elderly lady stepped forward.

"Reading stops me from feeling lonely," she said. "I like mystery stories but I don't know which one to choose."

"Why are you bothering me about it?" Jack Frost said. "Go and look through the shelves like everyone else. Next!"

"Oh, I can't bear it," said Jude with a little sob. "Librarians should always have time to help people. Our job is about so much more than putting books on shelves. If we don't stop him, people will start to think that all librarians are rude and unhelpful. Then they'll stop coming to libraries, and Jack Frost will have won!"

Chapter Nine
Testing Jack Frost

"We have to find a way to get those glasses away from Jack Frost," said Rachel.

"That won't be easy while he's wearing them," said Kirsty.

As they watched, the Ice Lord wrote the wrong name on a girl's new library card.

"Stop moaning," he snapped, when she pointed out his mistake.

"Excuse me, are you going to start a children's book club?" asked a boy. "I'd love to join."

"Why would I want to do something like that?" asked Jack Frost, wrinkling up his nose as if he had noticed a bad smell. "That's not my job! I'm here to shout at people and tell them what to do."

The little boy looked disappointed, and Jude put her face in her hands.

"He has no idea what a librarian does," she said, groaning. "He's going to make all these children scared of librarians. But librarians are supposed to be friendly and helpful, and help children learn to love books."

"Maybe we should teach him what

this job is really all about," said Rachel.
"It might help us get close to the radiant
reading glasses too. I've got an idea, but
we're going to need a disguise. Jack Frost
would recognise us."

Jude thought for a moment, and then a
smile spread across her face.

"Jack Frost never looks at human
beings very closely," she said. "I think a
change of hair would be
enough to fool him."

She gave a gentle
tap of her wand on
each girl's head. At
once, Kirsty's long,
dark hair changed to
a fiery red bob, and
Rachel's blonde curls
became a chocolate-

brown pixie cut. The girls giggled as they looked at each other.

"It really makes you look different," said Kirsty.

"You too," said Rachel. "Come on, let's see if we can show Jack Frost what a good librarian should be able to do."

First, Kirsty went up and tapped Jack Frost on the shoulder.

"Excuse me, could you help me?" she

said. "Can you show me a book that would be good for a four-year-old who is just learning to read?"

"How should I know?" Jack Frost growled. "I'm here to organise things, not read to annoying human brats."

"Oh, but you clever librarians don't just organise things," said Kirsty with a smile. "You help people to discover the magic of books."

Jack Frost screwed up his face and pretended to be sick. Rachel hurried forward.

"Please, can you help me?" she asked. "Could you search for a book I want to read? It's very hard to find."

"I could," said Jack Frost. "But I won't.
That sounds too much like hard work."

"But that's not hard work for a
wonderful librarian like you," said
Rachel. "Librarians can always find any
book, no matter how rare it is."

Jack Frost folded his arms and glared.

"That's not the sort of librarian I am,"
he muttered grumpily.

Just then, Alana Yarn came up to him.

"Are you one of the librarians?" she asked. "I was wondering what time you would like me to do my reading."

"I haven't organised that," Jack Frost yelled, flapping his hands at her. "Ugh, I wish everyone would stop asking me questions. Leave me alone!"

Chapter Ten
A Little Help from Alana Yarn

For a moment, the girls thought Jack Frost might storm out. But he touched the glasses he was wearing and took some deep breaths.

"The radiant reading glasses are helping him to calm down and organise his thoughts," Jude whispered.

"Who are you, anyway?" Jack Frost asked Alana Yarn.

"I'm an author," she replied.

"She's an amazing author," added Rachel.

"Lots of people are coming just to hear her read aloud," said Kirsty. "And it's all been organised by Wetherbury's wonderful librarian."

"Well, I don't want to be a librarian any more," said Jack Frost. "And I don't want everyone staring at her. I want to be the famous author."

He pushed the radiant reading glasses up his nose and glared at Alana Yarn. Then he ran over to the big yellow armchair in the middle of the library, shoving people out of the way as he went. He plonked himself down as if the

98

chair were his throne.

"Don't I look perfect?" he asked, letting his spiky hair out of the topknot. "This is just the right sort of outfit for an author to wear, and my glasses show how clever I am. I'm going to be so famous and successful, just you wait and see."

"You can't sit there," said Rachel, following him. "That's where Alana Yarn is going to do her reading."

"That's OK," said Alana Yarn in a gentle voice.

She patted Rachel's shoulder and bent down beside Jack Frost.

"You know, it doesn't matter what you wear," she said. "When you're an author, it's your words that matter most. Be yourself. For example, glasses don't really make you look clever. You should only wear them if you actually need them."

Suddenly, Rachel had a wonderful idea.

"Get ready to magic up an identical pair of glasses," she whispered to Jude.

Then she bent down next to Jack Frost, just like Alana Yarn.

"Alana is right," she said. "Let's see

what you look like without the glasses."

Before Jack Frost could say a word, she had plucked the glasses off with her right hand and whipped them around behind her back. Instantly, Jude waved her wand, and another pair of glasses appeared in Rachel's left hand.

"You can keep your silly advice," said Jack Frost. "Give those back!"

Rachel held out the glasses in her left hand. Jack Frost snatched them, jumped out of the chair and stuck out his tongue.

"I think I've done everything I came

for," he said, looking around at the confusion with a smile. "I've got plenty of other libraries to visit."

He stomped away, and the girls huddled together in excitement, holding the real radiant reading glasses between them.

"Thank goodness!" Rachel whispered.

"Jack Frost didn't notice a thing!" said

Kirsty, holding the glasses out to Jude.

Jude fluttered out from under Kirsty's hair and the glasses shrank to fairy size as soon as she touched them.

"As soon as I return these to the Fairyland Library, things should start looking a lot more organised here," she whispered. "Thank you, girls. You're the best friends any fairy could wish for."

She disappeared in a twinkling of tiny lights, which wafted into Rachel and Kirsty's hair, and returned them to their normal selves again. Just then, the blonde librarian came up to them with a box. She was wearing a huge smile.

"I found the medals!" she said when she saw the girls. "Now we can get on with our next events – the Reading Challenge awards and the reading from Alana

Yarn. I'll just go and ask for some help to tidy up the books on the floor. That new librarian has some rather . . . er . . . unusual ways."

"Oh, I think he's gone," said Kirsty.

The librarian looked very relieved.
"It's probably for the best," she said.
"Where did you find the medals?"
Rachel asked.

"It was the strangest thing," said the
librarian. "I had just checked the storage
cupboard, and it was empty. Then I
opened it again and the box was right in

front of me. It was like magic!"

Rachel and Kirsty smiled. The librarian had no idea how right she was!

Story Three
The Brilliant Bookmark

Chapter Eleven
Mops and Magic

Wetherbury Library was soon neat and tidy again. The librarian stood up and clapped her hands together.

"I am delighted to say that it is time for the Reading Challenge awards," she said.

Rachel and Kirsty joined a group of

excited children. They had each read five books to complete the reading challenge.

"You should all be very proud of your reading," said the librarian. "I have a special award for each of you. Please come forward when I call your name."

Each child was given a little red box. When it was Kirsty's turn, she opened the box and saw a golden medal with the word 'reader' printed on it.

"Wow, that's lovely," she said. "Thank you."

Next, the librarian called Rachel's name. Rachel took her box, and as she began to open it, she saw a silvery sparkle inside.

"Magic," she whispered, tingling with excitement. "Kirsty, I think Jude might be inside my medal box."

"Oh good," said Kirsty. "Let's find somewhere safe to talk to her."

The girls looked around.

"There's a cupboard," said Rachel. "Let's hide in there."

The girls slipped into the cupboard among mops and buckets. They left the door open a crack. Then Rachel held up her medal box and opened the lid. Jude sprang out and twirled into the air.

"Welcome back," said Kirsty, smiling.

"Have you come to ask us to help find the brilliant bookmark?"

Jude nodded.

"I followed Jack Frost after he left here," she said. "He went straight to the library in Tippington. When he realised that he didn't have the radiant reading glasses any more, he was furious. He gave the brilliant bookmark to one of his goblins, and sent him here to spoil things for everyone."

"You mean he's somewhere here in the library?" asked Rachel.

Jude nodded again, looking anxious.

"We'll find him," said Kirsty in a confident voice. "Jude, can you turn us into fairies so we can search?"

Jude waved her wand, and once again the girls heard the sound of ruffling pages. A hazy mist of fairy dust surrounded them, sparkling in the dim light. Then they were fairies again, fluttering filmy wings.

"Let's hurry," said Jude. "The brilliant bookmark keeps all the books in the right places on the shelves. With a goblin in charge of it, things could be about to get very muddled indeed."

The fairies left the cupboard and zigzagged across the library. They spotted the goblin almost at once. He was running down one of the aisles, holding something sparkly.

"That's my bookmark," said Jude. "He's using it to mix up all the books. The librarian's work is being ruined!"

Chapter Twelve
Disaster Strikes

Rachel looked around and saw that there was no one else in the aisle. She swooped down and hovered in front of the goblin. He jumped backwards in surprise, tripped over and fell down on his bottom.

"Leave me alone," he squawked. "Pesky little fairy."

"That bookmark doesn't belong to you," said Rachel.

The goblin blew a raspberry at her.

"You can't stop me," he yelled.

He scrambled up and ran out of the building. Just then, people started calling out to the librarian.

"Excuse me," said one voice. "Why are all the fiction books in the cookery section?"

"The children's books are filed under history," said another.

"I can't find any travel books," grumbled someone else. "What a shambles the shelves are."

"We need a good librarian," said a loud voice.

"This is terrible," said Kirsty. "The lovely librarian will get the blame for everything that naughty goblin has done."

"We have to stop him and put this right," said Jude.

The fairies zoomed after the goblin. Outside, they saw him halfway to the village shops. People turned to stare as he barged past them. The horses up at Bramble Stables leaned over their fence and whinnied.

"We have to catch up with him," said Rachel.

"Where is he going?" Kirsty said, panting. "I don't think I can fly this fast for much longer."

The goblin ran past the play park, raced past the shops and swerved to the left.

"Oh no," said Kirsty. "He's going into the museum."

The goblin darted inside the old red-brick building. The door slammed shut behind him.

"The museum library is full of rare

books," said Kirsty in alarm.

"How can we get in?" asked Jude. "The door is shut and there are no windows open."

"The village has been trying to raise money to repair the tiles on the museum roof," said Kirsty, flying upwards. "We can get in that way."

The fairies landed beside one of the broken tiles. There was a dark hole in the roof and Kirsty fluttered slowly in.

"I hope I can find the way," she whispered. "If we're too slow, the rare books could be in real danger."

Kirsty led Rachel and Jude into a dark, cobwebby roof space, and then down through some cracks between the floorboards. Below them, an elderly man was talking to a group of people. The fairies perched on a wooden rafter.

"There's the museum librarian with a tour group," said Kirsty. "But where is the goblin?"

Chapter Thirteen
Through the Door

Chapter Thirteen
Through the Roof

The tour group was standing in front of a large glass case filled with books.

"How unusual," said Rachel. "That child is wearing a frilly baby bonnet."

"This is our collection of books about Wetherbury," said the librarian. "Some of these titles are over two hundred years old. They are so rare that these are the only copies left in the world."

He turned to look at his group and jumped in surprise.

"Good heavens, that bonnet is from our costume collection," he said. "You should not be wearing that, young man. Please give it back."

"Shan't!" the child snapped in a squawking voice.

The fairies exchanged looks of alarm.

"That's the goblin," cried Jude.

"And he's standing next to the books," said Rachel.

The goblin raised his hand, and the fairies saw the magical bookmark sparkling.

"If he muddles those books up roughly, they will be ruined," Kirsty exclaimed.

128

"Can't he see how special they are?"

"That gives me an idea," said Rachel. "If he can't see them, he can't harm them. Jude, turn out the lights!"

Jude waved her wand, and instantly the museum went dark. The fairies felt for each other's hands.

"Good heavens," said the librarian again. "We must have had a power cut."

"Let me out of here," wailed the goblin. "I'm scared of the dark!"

There were a few cries and yelps of surprise.

"I bet he's pushing people out of the way, trying to reach the door," said Kirsty. "Thank goodness he didn't get to those books. Let's fly back out and stop him as he leaves."

"But how?" asked Rachel. "It's pitch black and I can't see my own hands. We'll never find the way out."

In the darkness, Jude whispered the words of a spell. At once, the tip of her wand glowed with a blue-green light.

"Come on," she whispered.

They flew back up through the cracks

into the roof space, and then through the broken tiles and into the sunlight. Smiling, Jude blew on the tip of her wand, and the light went out like a candle. Kirsty was already zooming towards the museum door. It burst open and the goblin stumbled out.

"You pesky fairies!" he screeched when he saw them flying towards him. "You've spoiled all my fun."

Then he turned and sprinted away. Jude quickly turned the lights of the museum back on, and then the fairies chased after the goblin. Still in the frilly bonnet, he ran past the shoppers, past the park, up the hill and into the woods behind Bramble Stables.

"We'll lose him in there," said Jude.

"Oh no we won't," Rachel promised. "Kirsty knows these woods."

The fairies weaved between the trees with Kirsty in the lead. The dappled light made it hard to see clearly. But Kirsty often played in the woods, and she knew all the trees. As she flew past a young oak tree, she paused.

"I've never noticed that branch before," she said. "It's a strange shape."

The branch moved, and its leaves trembled.

"That's not a branch at all," cried Kirsty. "That's the goblin!"

Chapter Fourteen
The Goblin Tree

The goblin was clinging to the trunk and sticking out his bony arms to look like branches. The trembling leaves were the frills of his bonnet.

"You dratted fairies," he grumbled. "Why can't you let me have some fun?"

"You could have really damaged the

museum's old books," said Jude.

"Pah, who cares about old books?" the goblin jeered.

"Librarians do," said Jude.

"And we do," Rachel added.

"And so does anyone who loves reading and learning," said Kirsty, hoping to make him understand. "Every book you pick up takes you into another world. It teaches you things and takes you on adventures. Books are precious."

The goblin stared at her with his mouth open.

"That's one of the reasons why librarians are so important," said Rachel. "They look after all these precious books for us. They help us find the stories that we'll love best."

"Please," said Jude, holding out her

hands. "If you can't be a friend to fairies, be a friend to librarians. If Jack Frost keeps that bookmark, no one will be able to find the right book for them. Can you imagine a world without books?"

The goblin shuffled down the tree and the fairies fluttered down beside him. When he was on the ground, he glared at them.

"You can't stop me, you bunch of goody two-shoes," he said. "I've got my orders. Jack Frost told me to mess things up for librarians, libraries and book lovers. So that's what I'm going to do."

He pulled a horrible face at them under the bonnet. Then he turned and ran.

"Oh no, not again," cried Kirsty.

They chased the goblin back through

the woods and down the hill. He was almost back at the library when he stumbled and fell head over heels.

"Yowch!" he squawked.

The fairies fluttered down beside him. Jude instantly turned Rachel and Kirsty back into humans. The best friends took one arm each and helped the goblin to his feet.

"Ow!" he wailed at once. "My ankle!"

"Jude, can you heal it?" Rachel asked.

"I don't know enough first aid," said Jude, looking upset. "What shall we do?"

"I know," said Kirsty. "Go to Fairyland and ask Martha the Doctor Fairy to come."

"Good thinking," said Rachel. "We'll help the goblin to the library. I'm sure they'll have an ice pack for his ankle."

Jude disappeared in a puff of silvery mist.

"OK, Mr Goblin," said Kirsty in a kind voice. "Let's find you somewhere to sit down."

With the goblin's arms around their necks, Rachel and Kirsty helped him to walk to the library. It was still busy and noisy. Some people were speaking crossly

140

to the librarian. She looked pale and worried.

The girls helped the goblin to sit down in an armchair. He clutched his ankle.

"Oh poor me, poor me," he whimpered. "I'm so unlucky. My mum warned me

about hanging around with humans. I wish I'd listened."

"Perhaps she should have warned you about Jack Frost," said Rachel.

"We need something to take his mind off his ankle," said Kirsty, looking around. "Aha!"

One of Alana Yarn's books was lying on

the floor beside her and she picked it up.

"I'll read to you until Martha gets here," she said.

Chapter Fifteen
Fairy First Aid

Kirsty was good at reading aloud. She did all the voices. The goblin stopped complaining about his ankle. He leaned closer and closer to Kirsty.

"Please stop breathing in my ear," she said after a while. "It's ever so tickly."

"But I can't hear properly," the goblin

wailed. "This place is too noisy."

"That's because you've still got Jude's brilliant bookmark," Rachel said. "People are shouting because they can't find the books they want."

Just then, a magical light glowed under the goblin's chair. The girls knelt down to make a little shelter. Then Jude fluttered out with Martha the Doctor Fairy.

"Hello, girls," said Martha, tying back
her red-gold hair. "Now, where's my
patient?"

"It's good to see you, Martha," said
Kirsty. "Here he is."

Martha smiled at the goblin and ran
her tiny hands over his ankle. Then she
nodded to herself.

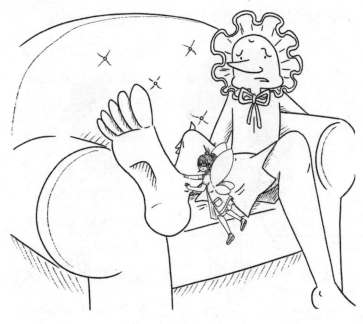

"I can mend this in a twinkle," she said. "I just need to get you back to my surgery in Fairyland."

"But I want to hear the end of the chapter," the goblin cried. "Please!"

"You won't be able to hear anything with all this noise going on," Rachel reminded him.

The goblin looked down at the bookmark. Then he shoved it towards Jude. As soon as it touched her, the bookmark shrank to fairy size. She pressed it to her chest.

"Thank you," she said, smiling up at
the goblin.

At once, the angry voices in the library
grew softer and quieter. Kirsty started to
read again.

Meanwhile, Jude got to work. Now that
she had her brilliant bookmark back,

it was easy to put all the library books back where they belonged. The visitors suddenly forgot why they had been so cross. People started to smile again.

"It's time for us to go," said Martha, when Kirsty had finished the chapter.

"Girls, I hope we'll see you in Fairyland soon."

"We hope so too," said Kirsty.

She and Rachel stood up to hide the goblin from sight. They blinked, and he and Martha vanished. Then they squeezed into the armchair together and held Jude in their cupped hands.

"Rachel, Kirsty, how can I thank you enough?" said the little fairy. "I would never have my magical objects back without your help."

"We're so glad that everything is back to normal for librarians," said Rachel.

"Now I must go," Jude told them with a smile.

"Goodbye," whispered the girls.

Jude disappeared, and the girls heard the librarian's voice.

"Thank you for your patience," she said. "I am pleased to introduce the famous author Alana Yarn."

The girls hurried to join the crowd around Alana's chair.

"I wonder when we'll visit Fairyland again," whispered Kirsty, as Alana opened her book.

"For now, I'm happy to be right here," Rachel replied. "I think human libraries are pretty magical places too!"

The End

**Now it's time for Kirsty and
Rachel to help ...**

Olympia the Games Fairy

Read on for a sneak peek ...

"This is going to be really exciting!"
Kirsty Tate said, beaming at her best
friend, Rachel Walker. Kirsty had just
arrived in Tippington to stay with
Rachel for part of the summer holidays.
"It's the first time I've ever been to a –
a –" Kirsty stopped, looking confused.
"*What* did you say this sporting event
was called, Rachel?"

Her friend laughed. "A triathlon," she
reminded Kirsty as Mr Walker turned the
car down a street signposted *To the river.*
"All the athletes take part in swimming,
cycling and running races, one after the

other. They don't even get a break in between! That's right, isn't it, Mum?"

"Yes," replied Mrs Walker from the passenger seat. "They go from one event straight into the next."

Kirsty's eyes opened wide. "Wow, they must be super-fit!" she exclaimed.

"I think we're going to be exhausted just cheering them on," joked Mr Walker, who was now searching for an empty space in the packed car park.

The triathlon was taking place in the pretty riverside town of Melford, not far from Tippington. As they all climbed out of the car, Kirsty admired the little thatched cottages and the stone-built church with its square bell tower. It was a perfect summer's day with a brilliant-blue sky and sunshine streaming down.

"There are loads of people here,"

Rachel remarked, as they followed the crowds down the street. Ahead of them the girls could see a long waterfront with an ancient stone bridge spanning the wide river. A set of steps led down to the edge of the river, and there were men and women in swimming costumes and colourful swimming caps standing on the steps, waiting eagerly for the race to start.

Read Olympia the Games Fairy to find out what adventures are in store for Kirsty and Rachel!

Calling all parents, carers and teachers!
The Rainbow Magic fairies are here to help
your child enter the magical world of reading.
Whatever reading stage they are at, there's
a Rainbow Magic book for everyone!
Here is Lydia the Reading Fairy's guide to
supporting your child's journey at all levels.

Starting Out

Our Rainbow Magic Beginner Readers are perfect for first-time readers who are just beginning to develop reading skills and confidence. Approved by teachers, they contain a full range of educational levelling, as well as lively full-colour illustrations.

Developing Readers

Rainbow Magic Early Readers contain longer stories and wider vocabulary for building stamina and growing confidence. These are adaptations of our most popular Rainbow Magic stories, specially developed for younger readers in conjunction with an Early Years reading consultant, with full-colour illustrations.

Going Solo

The Rainbow Magic chapter books - a mixture of series and one-off specials - contain accessible writing to encourage your child to venture into reading independently. These highly collectible and much-loved magical stories inspire a love of reading to last a lifetime.

www.orchardseriesbooks.co.uk

"Rainbow Magic got my daughter reading chapter books. Great sparkly covers, cute fairies and traditional stories full of magic that she found impossible to put down" - Mother of Edie (6 years)

"Florence LOVES the Rainbow Magic books. She really enjoys reading now" - Mother of Florence (6 years)

Read along the Reading Rainbow!

Well done – you have completed the book!

This book was worth 2 stars.

See how far you have climbed on the Reading Rainbow opposite.
The more books you read, the more stars you can colour in
and the closer you will be to becoming a Royal Fairy!

Do you want to print your own Reading Rainbow?

1) Go to the Rainbow Magic website

2) Download and print out the poster

3) Colour in a star for every book you finish
and climb the Reading Rainbow

4) For every step up the rainbow,
you can download your very own certificate

There's all this and lots more at
orchardseriesbooks.co.uk

You'll find activities, stories, a special newsletter
AND you can search for the fairy with your name!